For Flo, Tommy, Lucas and Hugo

M.D.

For Sylvie who inspires amazing stories and could have been the little girl in this book

L.B.

MYRIAD BOOKS LIMITED
35 Bishopsthorpe Road, London SE26 4PA

First published in 2003 by
MIJADE PUBLICATIONS
16-18, rue de l'Ouvrage, 5000 Namur-Belgium

© Laurence Bourguignon, 2003
© Michaël Derullieux, 2003

Translation: Lisa Pritchard

ISBN 1 84746 039 9

Printed in China

The three monsters
big night out

Laurence Bourguignon and Michaël Derullieux

MYRIAD BOOKS LIMITED

One night, three sad monsters sat by the fire.

"Nobody remembers us," said Hairy.
"Nobody tells our story any more," said Spike.
"Let's go up and see what's going on," said Two-Horns.

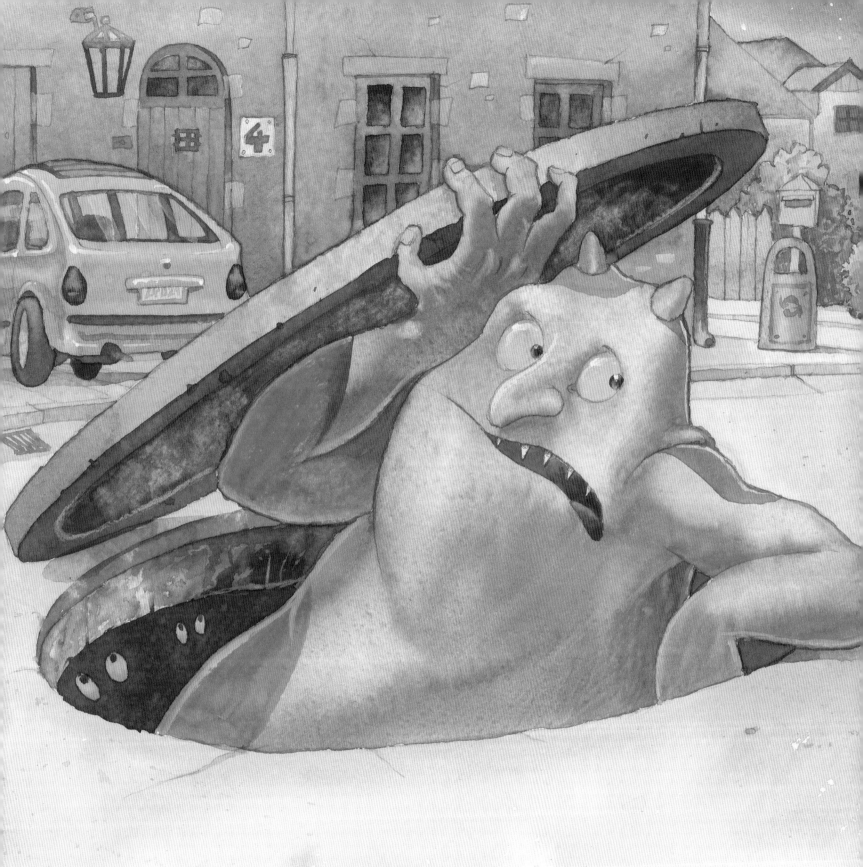

The three monsters followed the tunnel up
and climbed out into the street.

Nobody was in the street because it was very late. All the children had gone to bed, and their mums and dads were reading bedtime stories to them.

"I want to hear the story!" said Two-Horns. So they tiptoed up, and Spike climbed up on to Two-Horns' shoulders. He looked in at the window.

But there were no monsters in that story – just a sweet little kangaroo.

The three monsters went to every house and listened at all the windows.

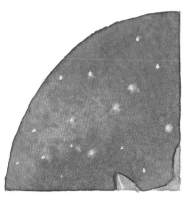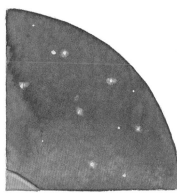
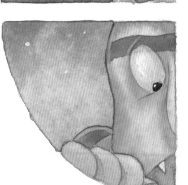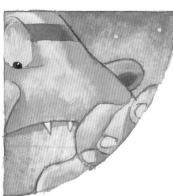

But it was the same everywhere. All the stories were sweet. None were about monsters.

The three monsters were very sad. They sat down to think.

"I've got an idea," said Two-Horns.

"Let's make lots of noise!"

So the three monsters started making a terrible din.
Two-Horns biffed the dustbin. BANG BING BONG!
Spike wailed and moaned. AAARGH UURGH
AAAARGH!

Hairy rang the doorbell at every house.
RING! RING RING!
But nobody came out.

The three monsters sighed.
Nobody believed in monsters
any more.
"Maybe we should just go
back home," said Spike.

But Two-Horns saw another window.
"We didn't try that one!" he said.
"It'll be like all the others," said Spike.
"Let's give it a try," said Two-Horns.

Two-Horns climbed up a tree and looked in through the window.

He saw a little girl. She was drawing something. He looked at the paper.

She was drawing a monster with horns, just like him! He leaned over
to see better and his horns knocked the window. Oops!

The little girl looked up and saw him.

Down below Spike and Hairy were getting tired of waiting.

"Hurry up, Two-Horns!" they shouted.

When he didn't answer they climbed up to see what was going on.

They climbed in through the open window.
There was Two-Horns sitting beside
a little girl. He was very happy.
"Look, she's making up a story about
monsters – and we are the monsters!"
he said.

"That's great," said Hairy. "Tell us the story."

When they were sitting comfortably, the little girl began:
"Well, these three monsters were very cross because nobody liked them any more. They met a little girl who still believed in them. They were so happy they gave her a present. But I don't know what…"

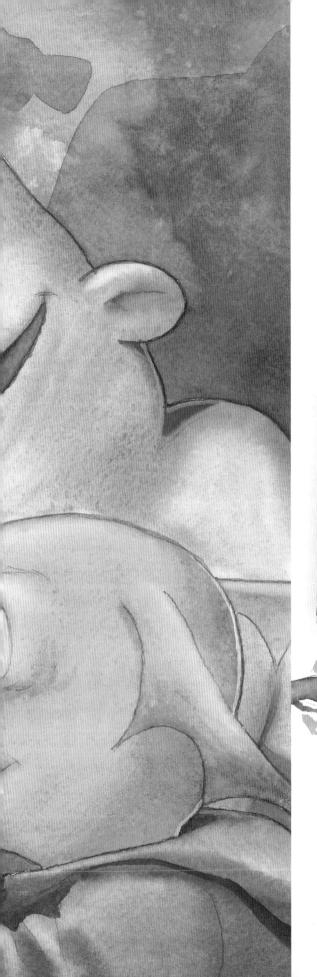

"I know!" said Two-Horns. "I'll give you one of my horns."

"And I'll give you a hair," said Hairy.

"And I'll give you a spiky claw," said Spike.

"Thank you," said the little girl. "I'll keep them for ever."

Before they left, the three monsters all gave her a hug.

"Don't forget us!" they said.

"I won't!" said the little girl.

It didn't take the monsters long to get home. Two-Horns itched his head where his new horn was already growing.
"Was it all a dream?" he said. "Did it really happen?"

"It wasn't a dream," said Hairy. "Look!"
There in his hand was the little girl's drawing of the three monsters.

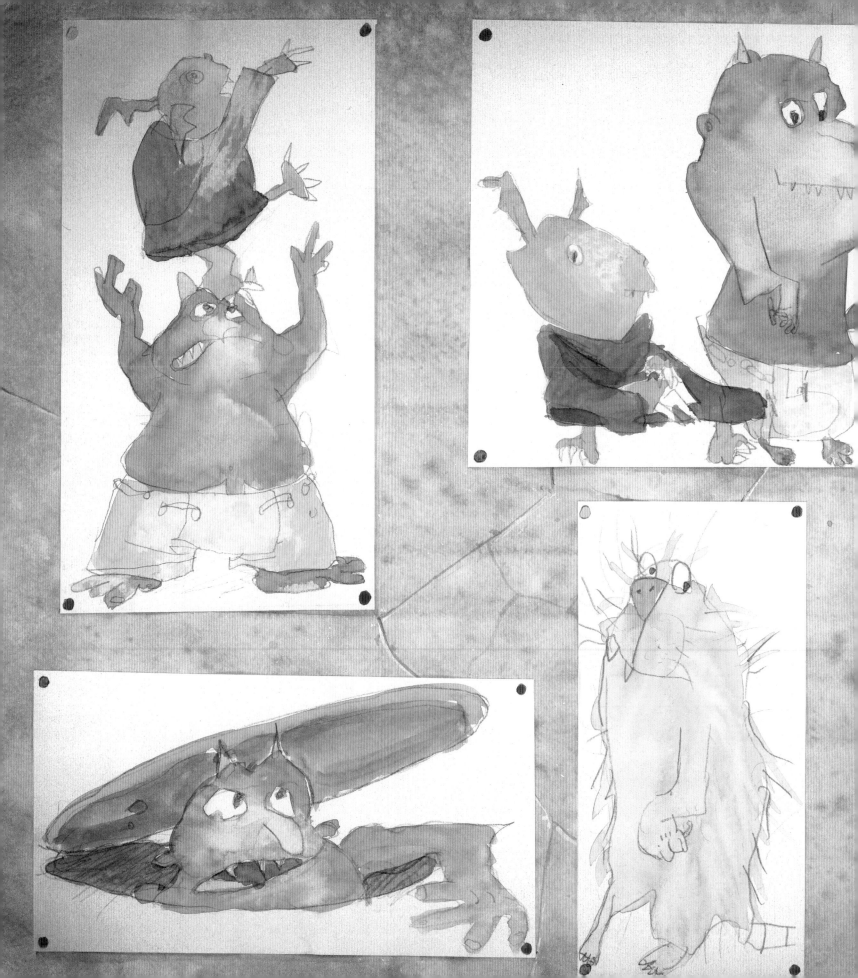